PUFFIN BOOKS

EDITOR: KAYE WEBB

MRS PEPPERPOT TO THE RESCUE

In the ordinary way Mrs Pepperpot was just a little old
woman whose children had grown up and gone away,
and who stayed at home keeping house for her husband.
But there was one odd thing about her – the way she
would suddenly shrink till she was no bigger than a
pepperpot.

Once she had shrunk she wasn't ordinary at all.
She was small enough to go to school in Rita's satchel
and help her make coffee for the teachers, small enough
to hide in the cat basket with the kittens, small enough to
ride on a rocket on Midsummer Eve, and small enough
to play matchbox cars with the baby mice in her cupboard. And these are some of the adventures she has in
this book.

Mrs Pepperpot is already a firm favourite with readers
who have the other Puffin books, *Little Old Mrs Pepperpot*,
and *Mrs Pepperpot in the Magic Wood*.

ALF PRØYSEN

Mrs Pepperpot to the Rescue

AND OTHER STORIES

TRANSLATED BY MARIANNE HELWEG
ILLUSTRATED BY BJÖRN BERG

PENGUIN BOOKS

BY ARRANGEMENT WITH HUTCHINSON OF LONDON

Penguin Books Ltd, Harmondsworth, Middlesex, England
Penguin Books Australia Ltd, Ringwood, Victoria, Australia

—

This translation first published by Hutchinson 1963
Published in Puffin Books 1968
Reprinted 1969, 1970, 1971 (twice), 1972 1973

—

Copyright © Alf Prøysen, 1960
Translation copyright © Hutchinson & Co. (Publishers) Ltd, 1963

—

Made and printed in Great Britain by
Cox & Wyman Ltd
London, Reading and Fakenham
Set in Monotype Baskerville

Contents

Mrs Pepperpot to the Rescue

WHEN it is breaking-up day at the village school, and the summer holidays are about to begin, all the children bring flowers to decorate the school. They pick them in their own gardens or get them from their uncles and aunts, and then they carry their big bunches along the road, while they sing and shout because it is the end of term. Their mothers and fathers wave to them from the windows and wish them a happy breaking-up day.

But in one window stands a little old woman who just watches the children go by. That is Mrs Pepperpot.

She has no one now to wish a happy breaking-up day, for all her own children are long since grown up and gone away, and none of the young ones think of asking her for flowers.

At least, that's not quite true; I do know of one little girl who picked flowers in Mrs Pepperpot's garden. But that was several years ago, not long after the little old woman first started shrinking to the size of a pepperpot at the most inconvenient moments.

That particular summer Mrs Pepperpot's

garden was fairly bursting with flowers: there were white lilac with boughs almost laden to the ground, blue and red anemones on strong, straight stalks, poppies with graceful nodding yellow heads and many other lovely flowers. But no one had asked Mrs Pepperpot for any of them, so she just stood in her window and watched as the children went by, singing and shouting, on their way to the breaking-up day at school.

The very last to cross the yard in front of her house was a little girl, and she was walking, oh, so slowly, and carried nothing in her hands. Mrs

Pepperpot's cat was lying on the doorstep and greeted her with a 'Miaow!' But the little girl only made a face and said, 'Stupid animal!' And when Mrs Pepperpot's dog, which was chained to the wall, started barking and wagging his tail the little girl snapped, 'Hold your tongue!'

Then Mrs Pepperpot opened the window to throw a bone out to the dog and the little girl whirled round and shouted angrily, 'Don't throw that dirty bone on my dress!'

That was enough. Mrs Pepperpot put her hands

on her hips and told the little girl that no one had any right to cross the yard in front of her house and throw insulting words at her or her cat and dog, which were doing no harm to anybody.

The little girl began to cry. 'I want to go home,' she sobbed. 'I've an awful pain in my tummy and I don't want to go to the breaking-up party! Why should I go when I have a pain in my tummy?'

'Where's your mother, child?' asked Mrs Pepperpot.

'None of your business!' snapped the girl.

'Well, where's your father, then?' asked Mrs Pepperpot.

'Never you mind!' said the girl, still more rudely. 'But if you want to know why I don't want to go to school today it's because I haven't any flowers. We haven't a garden, anyway, as we've only been here since Christmas. But Dad's going to build us a house now that he's working at the ironworks, and then we'll have a garden. My mum makes paper flowers and does the paper round, see? Anything more you'd like to know? Oh well, I might as well go to school, I suppose. Teacher can say what she likes – I don't care! If *she'd* been going from school to school for three years she wouldn't know much either! So blow her and her flowers!' And the little girl stared defiantly at Mrs Pepperpot.

Mrs Pepperpot stared back at the little girl and then she said: 'That's the spirit! But I think I can help you with the flowers. Just you go out in the garden and pick some lilac and anemones and poppies and anything else you like. I'll go and find some paper for you to wrap them in.'

So the girl went into the garden and started picking flowers while Mrs Pepperpot went indoors for some paper. But just as she was coming back to the door she shrank!

Roly Poly! And there she was, tucked up in the paper like jam in a pudding, when the little girl came running back with her arms full of flowers.

'Here we are!' shouted the little girl.

'And here *we* are!' said Mrs Pepperpot as she disentangled herself from the paper. 'Don't be scared; this is something that happens to me from time to time, and I never know when I'm going to shrink. But now I've got an idea; I want you to pop me in your satchel and take me along with you to school. We're going to have a game with them all! What's your name, by the way?'

'It's Rita,' said the little girl who was staring at Mrs Pepperpot with open mouth.

'Well, Rita, don't just stand there. Hurry up and put the paper round those flowers. There's no time to lose!'

When they got to the school the breaking-up party was well under way, and the teacher didn't look particularly pleased even when Rita handed her the lovely bunch of flowers. She just nodded and said, 'Thanks.'

'Take no notice,' said Mrs Pepperpot from Rita's satchel.

'Go to your desk,' said the teacher. Rita sat down with her satchel on her knee.

'We'll start with a little arithmetic,' said the teacher. 'What are seven times seven?'

'Forty-nine!' whispered Mrs Pepperpot from the satchel.

'Forty-nine!' said Rita.

This made the whole class turn round and stare at Rita, for up to now she had hardly been able to count to thirty! But Rita stared back at them and smiled. Then she stole a quick look at her satchel.

'What's that on your lap?' asked the teacher. 'Nobody is allowed to use a crib. Give me your satchel at once!'

So Rita had to carry it up to the teacher's desk where it was hung on a peg.

The teacher went on to the next question: 'If we take fifteen from eighteen what do we get?'

All the children started counting on their fingers, but Rita saw that Mrs Pepperpot was sticking both her arms and one leg out of the satchel.

'Three!' said Rita before the others had had time to answer.

This time nobody suspected her of cheating and Rita beamed all over while Mrs Pepperpot waved to her from between the pages of her exercise book.

'Very strange, I must say,' said the teacher. 'Now we'll have a little history and geography. Which country is it that has a long wall running round it and has the oldest culture in the world?'

Rita was watching the satchel the whole time, and now she saw Mrs Pepperpot's head pop up again. The little old woman had smeared her face with yellow chalk and now she put her fingers in the corners of her eyes and pulled them into narrow slits.

'China!' shouted Rita.

The teacher was quite amazed at this answer, but she had to admit that Rita was right. Then she made an announcement.

'Children,' she said, 'I have decided to award a treat to the one of you who gave the most right answers. Rita gave me all the right answers, so she is the winner, and she will be allowed to serve coffee to the teachers in the staff-room afterwards.'

Rita felt very pleased and proud; she was so used to getting meals ready when she was alone at home that she was sure she could manage this all right. So, when the other children went home, she took her satchel from the teacher's desk and went out into the kitchen. But, oh dear, it wasn't a bit like home! The coffee-pot was far too big and the huge cake with icing on it was very different from the plate of bread-and-dripping she usually got ready for her parents at home. Luckily the cups and saucers and plates and spoons had all been laid out on the table beforehand. All the same, it seemed too much to Rita, and she just sat down and cried. In a moment she heard the sound of scratching from the satchel, and out stepped Mrs Pepperpot.

'If you're the girl I take you for,' said the little old woman, putting her hands on her hips, 'you won't give up half-way like this! Come on, just you lift me up on the table, we'll soon have this job done! As far as I could see from my hiding place, there are nine visiting teachers and your own Miss Snooty. That makes two cups of water and two dessertspoons of coffee per person – which makes twenty cups of water and twenty dessert-spoons of coffee in all – right?'

'I think so. Oh, you're wonderful!' said Rita, drying her tears. 'I'll measure out the water and coffee at once, but I don't know how I'm going to cut up that cake!'

'That'll be all right,' said Mrs Pepperpot. 'As far as I can see the cake is about ninety paces – my paces – round. So if we divide it by ten that'll make each piece nine paces. But that will be too big for each slice, so we'll divide nine by three and make each piece three paces thick. Right?'

'I expect so,' said Rita, who was getting a bit lost.

'But first we must mark a circle in the middle of

the cake,' went on Mrs Pepperpot. 'Li.
your hand, please.'

Rita lifted her carefully on to her hand.

'Now take me by the legs and turn me upside down. Then, while you swing me round, I can mark a circle with one finger in the icing. Right; let's go!'

So Rita swung Mrs Pepperpot round upside down and the result was a perfect little circle drawn right in the middle of the cake.

'Crumbs are better than no bread!' said Mrs Pepperpot as she stood there, swaying giddily and licking her finger. 'Now I'll walk right round the cake, and at every third step I want you to make a little notch in the icing with the knife. Here we go!

'One, two, three, notch!
One, two, three, notch!
One, two, three, notch!'

And in this way Mrs Pepperpot marched all round the cake, and Rita notched it so that it made exactly thirty slices when it was cut.

When they had finished someone called from the staff-room: 'Where's that clever girl with the coffee? Hurry up and bring it in, dear, then you can fetch the cake afterwards.'

Rita snatched up the big coffee-pot, which was boiling now, and hurried in with it, and Mrs Pepperpot stood listening to the way the teachers praised Rita as she poured the coffee into the cups with a steady hand.

After a while she came out for the cake. Mrs Pepperpot clapped her hands: 'Well done, Rita! There's nothing to worry about now.'

But she shouldn't have said that, for while she was listening to the teachers telling Rita again how clever she was, she suddenly heard that Miss Snooty raising her voice:

'I'm afraid you've forgotten two things, dear,' she said.

'Oh dear!' thought Mrs Pepperpot, 'the cream-jug and the sugar-bowl! I shall have to look and see if they are both filled.'

The cream-jug was full, but when Mrs Pepperpot leaned over the edge of the sugar-bowl she toppled in! And at the same moment Rita rushed in, put the lid on the sugar-bowl and put it and the cream-jug on a little tray. Then she turned round and went back to the staff-room.

First Mrs Pepperpot wondered if she should tell Rita where she was, but she was afraid the child might drop the tray altogether, so instead she

buried herself well down in the sugar-bowl and
hoped for the best.

Rita started carrying the tray round. But her
teacher hadn't finished with her yet. 'I hope you
remembered the sugar-tongs,' she said.

Rita didn't know what to say, but Mrs
Pepperpot heard the remark, and when the visiting
head teacher took the lid off, Mrs Pepperpot
popped up like a jack-in-the-box holding a lump
of sugar in her outstretched hand. She stared
straight in front of her and never moved an eyelid,
so the head teacher didn't notice anything odd.
He simply took the sugar lump and waved Rita on
with the tray. But his neighbour at the table looked
hard at Mrs Pepperpot and said: 'What very

curious sugar-tongs – I suppose they're made of plastic. Whatever will they think of next?' Then he asked Rita if she had brought them with her from home, and she said yes, which was strictly true of course.

After that everyone wanted to have a look at the curious sugar-tongs, till in the end Rita's teacher called her over.

'Let me have a look at those tongs,' she said. She reached out her hand to pick them up, but this was too much for Mrs Pepperpot. In a moment

she had the whole tray over and everything fell on the floor. The cream-jug was smashed and the contents of the sugar-bowl rolled under the cupboard, which was just as well for Mrs Pepperpot!

But the teacher thought it was she who had upset the tray, and suddenly she was sorry she had been so hard on the little girl. She put her arms round Rita and gave her a hug. 'It was all my fault,' she said. 'You've been a very good little parlourmaid.'

Later, when all the guests had gone, and Rita was clearing the table, the teacher pointed to the dark corner by the cupboard and said, 'Who is that standing there?'

And out stepped Mrs Pepperpot as large as life and quite unruffled. 'I've been sent to lend a hand with the washing-up,' she said. 'Give me that tray, Rita. You and I will go out into the kitchen.'

When at last the two of them were walking home, Rita said, 'Why did you help me all day when I was so horrid to you this morning?'

'Well,' said Mrs Pepperpot, 'perhaps it was because you *were* so horrid. Next time maybe I'll help that Miss Snooty of yours. She looks pretty horrid too, but she might be nice underneath.'

Mrs Pepperpot on the Warpath

IT was the day after Mrs Pepperpot had helped Rita at the school party, and the little old woman was in a terrible rage. You see, if there's anything Mrs Pepperpot hates, it's people being unkind to children. All night she had been thinking about it, and now she had made up her mind to go and tell Rita's teacher just what she thought of her. So she put on her best hat and her best frock, straightened her back and marched off to the school.

'I hope I don't shrink this time,' she thought, 'but it's not likely to happen two days running. Anyway, today I must have my say or I shall

burst. Somebody's going to say she's sorry or my name's not Pepperpot!'

She had reached the school gate and swung it open. Then she walked up to the teacher's front door and knocked twice smartly. Then she waited.

No one said, 'Come in!'

Mrs Pepperpot knocked again, but there was still no answer. So she decided to try the latch. 'If the door isn't locked I shall go straight in,' she said to herself. She pressed the latch and the door opened. But no sooner had she put a foot over the threshold than she shrank and fell head over heels into a travelling-rug which was rolled up on the floor just inside the door! Next to it stood a suit-case and a hatbox.

'Oh, calamity!' cried Mrs Pepperpot, 'let's hope she's not in after all now!' But she was unlucky, for now she could hear footsteps in the corridor and the teacher came towards the front door dressed in her going-out clothes.

'What an old dolt I am!' thought Mrs Pepperpot. 'Fancy me not remembering the summer holidays have started today and she'll be going away, of course. Oh well, she's not gone yet. If I can manage to stay near her for a little while

longer I may still get my chance to give her a piece of my mind.' So she hid in the rug.

The teacher picked up the suitcase in one hand, then she threw the travelling-rug over her shoulder and picked up the hatbox in the other hand and walked out of the house, closing the door behind her. And Mrs Pepperpot? She was clinging for dear life to the fringe of the rug and she was still as angry as ever.

'Very nice, I must say!' she muttered. 'Going away on a holiday like this without a thought for

Rita and all the harm you did her. But you wait, my fine lady, very soon it'll be my turn to teach you a thing or two!'

The teacher walked briskly on, with Mrs Pepperpot dangling behind her, till they got to the station. Then she walked over to the fruit-stall and put the rug down on the counter, and Mrs Pepperpot was able to slip out of it and hide behind a bunch of flowers.

The teacher asked for two pounds of apples.

'That's right!' fumed Mrs Pepperpot to herself. 'Buy two pounds of apples to gorge yourself with on the train!'

'And eight oranges, please,' continued the teacher.

'Worse and worse!' muttered Mrs Pepperpot.

'And three pounds of bananas, please,' said the teacher.

Mrs Pepperpot could hardly contain herself: 'If I was my proper size now, I'd give you apples and oranges and bananas, and no mistake!'

Then the teacher said to the lady in the fruit-stall:

'Do you think you could do me a favour? I want all this fruit to go to one of my pupils, but I have to catch the train, so I've no time to take it to her myself. Could you deliver it to Rita Johansen in the little house by the church and tell her it's from me?'

On hearing this, Mrs Pepperpot's ears nearly fell off with astonishment. It was just as if someone had taken a sweet out of her mouth and left her nothing to suck; what was she going to say now?

'I'll do that for you with pleasure, miss,' said the fruit-lady. 'That'll be twelve shillings exactly.'

'Oh dear!' exclaimed the teacher, rummaging in her purse, 'I see I shan't have enough money left after buying my ticket. Would you mind if I owed you the twelve shillings till I come back from my holidays?'

'The very idea! Asking me to deliver goods you can't even pay for! I shall have to have the fruit back, please,' the fruit-lady said, and held out her hand.

The teacher said she was sorry, put the bag of fruit back on the counter and went off to board her train, but Mrs Pepperpot had taken the chance to jump into the bag.

Silently she wished the teacher a good holiday: 'You're not so bad after all, and you needn't worry; I'll see that Rita gets her bag of fruit some-how. But *somebody's* going to get the edge of my tongue before the day's out!'

Of course the fruit-lady could no more hear what Mrs Pepperpot was saying than the teacher could. She was busy getting ready to shut up shop and go home. But when she had put her hat on and opened the door she suddenly turned round and picked up the bag of fruit on the counter.

Mrs Pepperpot had just been wondering if she

was going to be locked in the fruit-stall all night, and now here she was, being taken on another journey!

'I suppose you're going to eat all this yourself, you selfish old thing, you!' thought Mrs Pepperpot, getting worked up again. 'The teacher may be snooty, but at least she has a kind heart underneath. You're just plain mean! But you just wait till I grow again!'

The fruit-lady walked on and on, until at last Mrs Pepperpot could hear her opening a door and going into a room. There she set the bag down with a thump on the table, and Mrs Pepperpot was able to climb over an orange and peep out of the top.

She saw a man banging on the table, and he was as cross as a sore bear. 'What sort of time is this to come home?' he roared. 'I've been waiting and waiting for my supper. Hurry up now! What's in that bag, anyway?'

'Oh, it's only some fruit for a little girl,' said his wife. 'The school-teacher wanted to send it to Rita Johansen, but she found she hadn't enough money, so I took it back. Then when she'd gone I felt sorry, so I thought I'd take it along to the child myself.'

This time Mrs Pepperpot was really amazed: 'Well, I never!' she gasped, 'here's another one who turns out to be nice. Still, I'm sure her husband won't; he looks as if he could do with a good ticking off!'

The fruit-lady's husband certainly was a cross-patch and no mistake. He banged his fist on the table and shouted that no wife of his was going to waste money and time running errands for silly school-teachers and brats.

'Give me that bag!' he roared. 'I'll take it right back to the shop this minute!' And he snatched up the bag from the table. Poor Mrs

Pepperpot was given an awful shaking and landed up jammed between two bananas.

Taking long strides, the man walked off down the road.

'Bye-bye, fruit-lady!' whispered Mrs Pepperpot. 'You have a nasty husband, but I'll deal with him shortly, don't you worry!'

Squeezed and bruised, the little old woman lay there in the bag while the man strode on. But after a while he walked more slowly and at last he stopped at a house and knocked on the door.

'Surely this isn't the station?' wondered Mrs Pepperpot.

She heard the door open and the man spoke: 'Are you Rita Johansen?'

Then she heard a little girl's voice, 'Yes, that's me.'

'Your teacher sent you this,' said the man and handed over the bag; 'it's fruit.'

'Oh, thank you!' said Rita. 'I'll just go and get a bowl to put it in.' And she set the bag on a chair.

'That's all right,' said the man, and he turned on his heel and walked away.

When Rita came back with the bowl she thought she heard the door close, but she didn't take much

notice in her eagerness to see what the teacher had sent her.

But it was actually Mrs Pepperpot who had slipped out, for she was now her usual size and she wanted time to think: it had all been so surprising and not at all what she expected. As she walked she began to hurry. For now she knew who was going to get a piece of her mind, and rightly so! Someone who made her more angry than anyone else just now!

When she got home she marched straight to the

mirror. Putting her hands on her hips she glared at the little old woman she saw there. 'Well!' she said, 'and who do you think you are, running round the country-side poking your nose in where you're not wanted? Is it any of your business, may I ask, who the school-teacher buys fruit for? What d'you mean by hiding in people's travelling-rugs and spying on them? You ought to be ashamed of yourself, an old woman like you, behaving like a senseless child. As for the fruit-lady, why shouldn't she be cross? How was she to know if she could trust the teacher? And her husband; I suppose he can bang his fist on his own table if he likes without you interfering? Are you listening? Wouldn't you be pretty mad if you'd come home hungry and the wife wasn't there to cook your meal, eh? I'm disgusted with you! *They* were sorry for what they did and made amends, all three of them, but *you*, you just stand there glaring at me as if nothing had happened. Wouldn't it be an idea to say you were sorry?'

Mrs Pepperpot turned her back on the mirror and took a deep breath. 'That's better!' she said. 'I've got it all off my chest at last. Now I can give my tongue a rest and get on with the housework.'

But first she took one more look in the mirror, smiled shyly and bobbed a little curtsy.

'I'm sorry!' she said.

And the little old woman in the mirror smiled back at her and bobbed a little curtsy too.

The Nature Lesson

EVERY morning, when Mrs Pepperpot sits at her window with her after-breakfast cup of coffee, she watches a little boy who always walks across her yard on his way to school. The boy's name is Olly and he and Mrs Pepperpot are very good friends, though not in the way grown-ups usually are friends with children. Quite often Olly rushes past Mrs Pepperpot's window without even saying 'Good morning', because he is in such a hurry. But then Mrs Pepperpot has never even asked him his name or how old he is or what he wants for Christmas. She just watches him every morning and says to herself, 'There goes the little boy on his way to school.' As for Olly, he just glances up at her window and thinks, 'There's the old woman, drinking her coffee.'

Now with animals it is different: if Olly sees the cat sitting on Mrs Pepperpot's doorstep he can't resist stopping to stroke her. He'll even sit down on the door-step and talk to her.

'Hello, pussy,' he'll say. 'There's a lovely pussy!' And then, of course, he has to go and see the dog outside his kennel as well, in case he should get jealous.

'Hullo, boy! Good dog, good dog! You didn't think I'd forgotten you, did you? Oh, I wouldn't do that! There's a good dog!' And by the time he's made a fuss of them both he's late for school.

This is Olly's trouble: he's *very* fond of animals. He loves to play hide-and-seek with the squirrel he sees on his way to school, or to have a whistling-match with a blackbird. And as for *rainy* days, well, he spends so much time trying not to step on the worms wriggling by the puddles in the road that he's *always* late for school.

This won't do, of course, and when he's late his teacher gets cross, and she'll say, 'It's all very well being fond of animals; it's quite right that you should be, but it's no excuse for being late for school.'

But that wasn't what I was going to tell you. What I was going to tell you was how Mrs Pepperpot had a nature lesson one day. So here we go!

It was a lovely spring day, and Mrs Pepperpot was sitting by the window as usual, enjoying her cup of coffee and watching Olly come across the yard. He was walking rather briskly this time – watching some bird or animal had probably made

him late again – so he had only time to say
'Hullo, puss!' to the cat on the door-step and 'Hi,
boy!' to the dog by the kennel.

But suddenly he stopped dead, turned round on
his heel and started running back across the yard.
Mrs Pepperpot had just come to the door to give
the dog his breakfast and Olly rushed past her as
fast as he could go.

Mrs Pepperpot called to him: 'Whatever's the
matter with you, boy? The police after you?'

'Forgot my nature textbook!' answered Olly
over his shoulder, and started off again.

'Wait a minute!' called Mrs Pepperpot. Olly
stopped. 'You can't go all the way home again
now; you'll be much too late for school. No, you
go on and *I'll* go back for your book and bring it
to you at school.'

Olly shuffled his feet a bit and looked unhappy;
he didn't much like the idea of an old woman
turning up in school with his nature textbook.

'Don't stand there shuffling, boy!' said Mrs
Pepperpot. 'Where did you leave the book?'

'On the window-sill,' he answered; 'the window
is open.'

'All right. Where do you want me to put the
book when I get to the school? Come on, hurry up;

we haven't got all day!' said Mrs Pepperpot, trying to look severe.

'There's a hole in the wall, just by the big birch tree; there's an old bird-nest there you can put it in.'

'In the old nest in a hole by the birch tree; right!' said Mrs Pepperpot. 'Now, off you go and see if you can be on time for a change! I'll see to the rest.'

'Righto!' said Olly and was off before you could say Jack Robinson.

Mrs Pepperpot took off her apron, smoothed her hair and stepped out into the yard. And then, of course, the inevitable thing happened; she shrank!

'This is bad,' thought Mrs Pepperpot, as she peeped over the wet grass by the door-step, 'but I've known worse.' She called to the cat: 'Come here, puss! You'll have to be my horse once again and help me fetch Olly's nature book from his house.'

'Miaow! All right,' said the cat, as she allowed Mrs Pepperpot to climb on her back. 'What sort of a thing is a nature book?'

'It's a book the children use in school to learn about animals,' answered Mrs Pepperpot, 'and one thing it says about cats is that you are "carnivores".'

'What does that mean?' asked the cat.

'That you eat meat, but never mind that now; all you have to do is to take me straight down the road till we get to the stream. Then we take a short cut across . . .'

But, as they came near the stream, the cat said, 'Doesn't the book say anything about cats not liking to get their feet wet?' And then she stopped so abruptly that poor Mrs Pepperpot toppled right over her head and fell plump into the water!

'Good job I can swim,' spluttered Mrs
Pepperpot as she came to the surface, 'humans
aren't meant to live under water on account of
the way they breathe with their lungs. Phew! It's
hard work all the same; I'll take a rest on this
stone and see if something turns up.'

While she was getting her breath a tiny animal
stuck its nose out of the water, and started snarling
at her. Now Mrs Pepperpot knew what that was,
but you probably wouldn't because it only lives
in the faraway places, and it is called a lemming.
Its fur is dappled brown and fawn, so that it looks
a bit like a guinea-pig in summer, but in winter it
turns white as the snow around it.

As I say, Mrs Pepperpot knew all about lemmings, so she snarled back at the little creature,
making as horrible a noise as she could. 'I'm not
afraid of you!' she said, 'though the book says

you're the worst-tempered of all the little rodents and don't give way to a fierce dog or even a grown man. But now you can just stop showing off and help me out of this stream like a good lemming.'

'Well, blow me down!' said the lemming. 'I never saw a woman as small as you and with such a loud voice. Get on my back and I'll take you across. Where are you going, by the way?'

'To fetch a nature book from the house over there for a little boy at school,' said Mrs Pepperpot. 'And in that book there is quite a bit about you.'

'Oh? And what does it say?' asked the lemming, crawling out on to the grass with Mrs Pepperpot.

'It says that once every so many years lemmings come down from the mountains in great swarms and eat up all the green stuff they can find till they get to the sea.' Then she stopped, because she remembered that when the lemmings reach the sea in their search for food, thousands of them get drowned.

'We do get rather hungry,' said the lemming; 'as a matter of fact, I'm on my way to join my mates in a little food-hunt . . .'

'Couldn't you just take me down to the house?' pleaded Mrs Pepperpot; she didn't like the idea that he might drown in the sea. But the lemming's empty tummy was telling him to go, so he told Mrs Pepperpot she would have to manage by herself, and he ran off muttering to himself about juicy green leaves.

Before Mrs Pepperpot had had time to wonder what would happen to him, another head appeared above a little wall. This time it was a stoat.

'Hullo, Mr Nosey Parker,' she greeted him, 'what are you looking for?'

'I thought you were a mouse, but I see you're a little old woman, and I don't eat women,' said the stoat. 'Have you by any chance got a silver spoon?' he added.

'I have something you like even better than silver spoons,' answered Mrs Pepperpot, 'a whole packet of tin-tacks, and you can have them if you'll take me to that house over there. I have to fetch a book from the window-sill for a little boy in the school.'

'All right,' said the stoat, 'hop up!'

So Mrs Pepperpot got on his back. But it was a most uncomfortable journey, because stoats, like weasels, move by rippling their long bodies, and though they have short legs, they can run very fast. Mrs Pepperpot had a job keeping on and was

glad when they reached the wall under the
window.

The stoat scrambled up the window-sill, and
presently he came back with the book – under his
chin.

'Why do you carry the book that way?' asked
Mrs Pepperpot.

'How else?' answered the stoat. 'I always
carry eggs under my chin.'

'Eggs?' Mrs Pepperpot pretended to be surprised. 'I didn't know stoats laid eggs.'

'Ha, ha, very funny!' said the stoat. 'I suppose
you don't eat eggs?'

'Oh yes,' said Mrs Pepperpot, 'but I don't steal them out of wild birds' nests.'

'That's my business,' said the stoat. 'Now you'd better think how you're going to get this book to school; I can't carry both you and the book.'

'That's true!' said Mrs Pepperpot. 'I'll have to think of something.'

But it wasn't necessary, for the next moment Mrs Pepperpot was back to her proper size. As she bent down to pick up the book she whispered to the little stoat, 'The tin-tacks will be waiting for you in that nest you robbed in the stone wall

by the school.' And she thought she heard him chuckle as he rippled away in the grass.

When she reached the school the bell was ringing for break, and she just had time to pop the book into the empty nest before Olly came running out with the other children. Mrs Pepperpot gave the tiniest nod in the direction of the wall and then she walked briskly away.

But the next morning Olly brought a lovely bone for her dog and from his milk bottle he poured a good saucer-full of milk for her pussy.

Mrs Pepperpot opened the window. 'Would you do something for me this morning?' she asked.

'As long as it won't make me late for school,' answered Olly.

'Good,' said Mrs Pepperpot. Then she fetched a packet of tin-tacks from the toolshed and gave them to Olly. 'Put those in the empty nest in the wall, will you? They're for a friend of mine.'

The Shoemaker's Doll

THERE was once a shoemaker who won a doll in a raffle at a bazaar. But a doll was no good to him living alone as he did in a little cottage where the floor was strewn with old soles and bits of leather and where everything he touched was covered in glue.

For, with all the village shoemaking to be done before he could do his own housework, you can imagine what the shoemaker's home looked like. And now there was this doll. When he had brought it home he stood looking round the little room and wondering where on earth he could put it. At last he decided to set the doll on top of the chest of drawers next to a half-loaf of bread and a rubber boot. Then he went to bed.

In the night he dreamed that the doll came over to his bed and said:

> *I can scrub, I can sweep,*
> *Make a bed and house-keep;*
> *If you won't, I will!*

When the shoemaker opened his eyes next morning and saw the doll on the chest of drawers he remembered the dream and laughed to himself.

'So you can scrub and sweep and make beds, can you, my little flibbertigibbet? Still, I suppose I had better do it myself to save you spoiling your pretty frock,' he said. So he made his bed, which hadn't been done properly for fifteen years, and underneath he found the old gold watch his grandfather had left him. Until that moment he thought it was lost for-ever. After that he washed the floor and found a half-crown lying in a corner behind the cupboard. Then he swept out all the rubbish from the drawer in his work-bench, and what do you think? Right at the bottom he found a little ring with a red stone in it!

At first the shoemaker was astonished, but then he remembered:

'Yes, yes, of course! It was that little girl from Crag House; she did tell me she had lost her ring here once. She came to ask me about it several times. I'll put it on the shelf here and give it to her when I see her. And now I suppose I'd better tidy up the chest of drawers for you, my little slave-driver!'

He started by removing the rubber boot. But he decided to leave the half-loaf, because he liked to take a bite from time to time while he was mending the shoes.

Later in the day a village woman came in. When she saw how tidy the room was she clapped

her hands and exclaimed: 'Well I never! What a change! You must have had a lot of time to spare getting the place so ship-shape. I suppose you have my shoes ready as well, then?'

The shoemaker pushed his spectacles up on his forehead and stared at the woman. Then he said, 'Come again Tuesday!'

'But it's Tuesday today,' objected the woman.

The shoemaker let his spectacles fall back on his nose.

'Come again Wednesday!' he snapped and went on with his work.

'Oh, you're just the same old lazy sour-puss that you always were!' said the woman, and left him to it.

In the afternoon a little boy started playing in the street outside the house. He came to the door and asked the shoemaker to button his jacket because his fingers were too cold to manage the buttonhole.

'Come again Thursday!' said the shoemaker in his snappy voice.

'But I'm cold today, mister!' said the little boy.

'Come again Friday!' said the shoemaker.

'You're just a grumpy old toad, so you are!' said the little boy, and went away.

'Good riddance!' said the shoemaker, and he didn't even turn round, but went on with his work, mending and patching till it was too dark to work any more. Then he ate up the rest of the loaf and climbed into bed. But in his sleep he dreamed that the doll came over to him and this is what she said:

> *'I can button, mend a hose,*
> *I can wipe a runny nose,*
> *If you won't, I will!'*

'You're a proper fusspot, aren't you?' said the shoemaker when he woke in the morning and remembered his dream. 'I'd better get those shoes finished for Mrs Butt. Then when I take them along to her I can take the ring for the little girl as well.'

So he sat down at his bench and finished mending Mrs Butt's shoes.

Meanwhile the little boy had started playing outside the window again; the shoemaker called him in.

'Come here, boy, let me button your coat for you,' he said. 'Would you like me to wipe that nose of yours too? You can tell me if it hurts.'

''Course it doesn't hurt,' said the little boy, blowing into the hankie like a trumpet and waving his fingers in the air; they were quite stiff and blue with cold. 'Not so cross today, are you?' he said, and then he added: 'I'd like to help *you* now. Got any messages for me to take?'

'Well yes, I have, as a matter of fact,' said the shoemaker. 'You can take these shoes to Mrs Butt at the corner, and while you're at it you can take this ring and give it to the little girl at Crag House; she lost it here a long time ago.'

'All right!' said the little boy and ran off with the things.

It wasn't long before he was back with a message from Mrs Butt. 'Mrs Butt told me to tell you that if you want your Sunday suit cleaned and pressed she'd be glad to do it for you. And that girl at Crag House told me to thank you and ask if you'd like to go to her birthday party tomorrow – she's asked me too, wasn't that nice of her?'

The shoemaker was staring in front of him, thinking hard. 'Very nice of her, I'm sure. But, as for me, I've been on my own for so long now I wouldn't know how to behave with other folks at a party. No, I'd better not go.'

But when the little boy had gone away and the shoemaker had got into bed he dreamed again that the doll came over to speak to him:

'*I always smile when folks are kind,*
Not turn my back and act so blind,
If you won't, I will!'

Next morning the shoemaker remembered and said to himself, 'I shall have to go, then.' And he has never regretted it. For one thing, he wore his Sunday suit, all neatly cleaned and pressed by Mrs Butt, and, for another, he had three different kinds of cake to eat, and, most important of all, he found that it is good for people to get together now and then and not always to be moping on their own.

Ever since that day the shoemaker's cottage has been as clean as a new pin, and the shoemaker himself whistles and sings as he goes about his housework. He makes his bed and scrubs the floor, he buttons boys' coats and wipes their noses and he mends the shoes in double-quick time.

Every now and again, when there's something he *doesn't* want to do, he takes a quick look at his doll on the chest of drawers, and he always ends up by doing whatever it is he has to do. For if *he* won't *she* will.

Mrs Pepperpot
is Taken for a Witch

MRS PEPPERPOT lives in a valley in Norway, and in summertime in that part of the world the nights hardly get dark at all. On Midsummer's Eve, in fact, the sun never quite goes down, so everybody, young and old, stays up all night to dance and sing and let off fireworks round a big bonfire. And because there's magic abroad on Midsummer's Eve they sometimes see witches riding on broomsticks through the sky – or they think they do, anyway.

Now the only people in that valley who never used to go to the bonfire party were Mr and Mrs Pepperpot. Not that Mrs Pepperpot didn't want to go, but Midsummer's Eve happened to be Mr Pepperpot's birthday as well, and on that day it was he who decided what they did. He never liked mixing with a crowd on account of that shrinking habit of Mrs Pepperpot; he was always afraid that she would suddenly turn the size of a pepperpot and disappear, leaving him standing there looking a proper fool.

But this year Mrs Pepperpot *did* go to the party, and this is how it happened.

It started the night before Midsummer's Eve. Mrs Pepperpot had been to the store and was walking slowly home with her basket on her arm. She was wondering how she could persuade her husband to go to the bonfire when suddenly she had an idea.

'I could ask him if there was something he really wanted for his birthday, and then I could say I would give it to him if he promised to take me to the bonfire party.'

As soon as she got inside the door she jumped on her husband's knee and gave him a smacking kiss on the tip of his nose.

'Dear, good hubby,' she said, 'have you got a very special wish for your birthday tomorrow?'

Her husband was quite surprised. 'Have you had sunstroke or something? How could you buy anything? Why, money runs through your fingers like water.'

'Sometimes it does, and sometimes it doesn't,' said Mrs Pepperpot, looking sly; 'there are such things as hens, and hens lay eggs and eggs can be sold. Just now I have quite a tidy sum put by, so just you tell me what you would like and the present will be laid out here on the table as sure as my name's Pepperpot.'

'Well,' he said, 'if you think you have enough money to buy that handsome pipe with the silver band that's lying in the store window, I'll promise you something in return.'

'Done!' cried Mrs Pepperpot at once, 'and the thing I want you to promise me is to take me to the bonfire party on Windy Ridge tomorrow night!'

So Mr Pepperpot had to agree and the next day Mrs Pepperpot filled her pockets with all the sixpennies, pennies and threepenny bits she had earned from the eggs and set off to the store.

'I want to buy the pipe with the silver band,'

said Mrs Pepperpot, when it came to her turn to be served.

But the grocer shook his head. 'Sorry, Mrs Pepperpot,' he said, 'but I'm afraid I sold that pipe to Peter Poulsen yesterday.'

'Oh dear,' said Mrs Pepperpot, 'I'll have to go and see if he'll let me buy it off him,' and she hurried out of the door, letting the door-bell jingle loudly as she went.

She took the shortest way to Peter Poulsen's house, but when she got there only his wife was at home.

'I was wondering if your husband would sell me that pipe he bought in the store yesterday?' said

Mrs Pepperpot. 'I'd pay him well for it,' she added, and patted her pocketful of coins.

'That pipe is no longer in the house,' said Mrs Poulsen, who had a sour look on her face. 'I wasn't going to have tobacco smoke in my curtains, no *thank* you! I gave it to some boys who were having a sale; they said they were collecting money for fireworks for tonight's bonfire, or some such nonsense.'

Mrs Pepperpot's heart sank; did Mrs Poulsen know where the sale was being held?

'Up on Windy Ridge, near the bonfire, the boys said,' answered Mrs Poulsen, and Mrs Pepperpot lost no time in making her way up to Windy Ridge.

But it was a tidy walk uphill and when she got to the top she found the boys had sold everything. They were busy tidying up the bits of paper and string and cardboard boxes and carrying them over to the bonfire.

Mrs Pepperpot was so out of breath her tongue was hanging out, but she managed to stammer, 'Who got the pipe?'

'What pipe?' asked one of the boys.

'The one with the silver band that Mrs Poulsen gave you.'

'Oh that,' said the boy; 'my brother bought it. But then he tried to smoke it and it made him sick. So he got fed up with it and tied it to a long pole and stuck it at the top of the bonfire. There it is – look!'

Mrs Pepperpot looked, and there it was, right enough, tied to a pole at the very top of the huge bonfire!

'Couldn't you take it down again?' she asked the boy.

'Are you crazy?' said the boy. 'Expect us to up-set the bonfire when we've got everything piled up

just nicely? Not likely! Besides, we're going to have some fun with that pipe; you wait and see! But I can't stand talking now, I must go and get a can of petrol to start it off.' And he ran off with the other boys.

'Oh dear, oh dear, oh dear!' wailed Mrs Pepperpot to herself. 'I see there's nothing for it but to climb that bonfire and get it down myself.' But she looked with dismay at the mountain of old mattresses, broken chairs, table-legs, barrows, drawers, old clothes and hats, car-tyres and empty cartons.

'First I shall have to find a stick to poke the pipe off the pole when I do get up aloft,' she thought.

Just at that moment she turned small, but for once Mrs Pepperpot was really pleased. 'Hooray!' she shouted in her shrill little voice. 'It won't take long for a little thing like me to get that pipe down now, and I don't even need to upset the bonfire!'

Quick as a mouse, she darted into the big pile and started climbing up from the inside. But it was not as easy as she had thought; climbing over a mattress she got her heel stuck in a spring and it took her quite a while to free herself. Then she had difficulty in climbing a slippery chair-leg; she kept sliding back. But at last she managed it, only to find herself entangled in the lining of a coat. She groped about in this for some time before she found her way out of the sleeve.

By now people had started gathering round the bonfire.

'All right, let them have a good look,' she thought. 'Luckily I'm too small for them to see me up here. And nothing's going to stop me from getting to the top now!'

Just then she lost her grip and fell into a deep drawer. There she lay, puffing and blowing, till she managed to catch hold of a bonnet string which was hanging over the edge of the drawer.

'Not much farther to go, thank goodness!' she told herself, but when she looked down she almost fainted; it was fearfully far to the ground, and now there were crowds of people standing round, waiting for the bonfire to be lit.

'No time to lose!' thought Mrs Pepperpot, and heaved herself on to the last obstacle. This was easy, because it was an old concertina, so she could walk up it like a staircase.

Now she was at the foot of the pole and at the top was the pipe, securely tied!

'However am I going to get up there?' she wondered, but then she noticed the rim of an empty tar-barrel right next to her. So she smeared a little tar on her hands to give them a better grip, and then she started to climb the pole. But the pole and the whole bonfire seemed to be heeling a little to one side, and when she looked down she nearly fell off with fright: *the boys had lit the bonfire!*

Little flames were licking up round the mattresses and the broken furniture.

Then people started cheering and the children chanted: 'Wait till it gets to the pipe at the top! Wait till it gets to the pipe at the top!'

'Catch me waiting!' muttered Mrs Pepperpot. 'I've got to get there *first*!' and she climbed on up till her hands gripped the stem of the pipe. Down below she could hear the children shouting:

'Watch the flames when they reach the pole! There's a rocket tied to the pipe!'

'Oh, good gracious!' cried Mrs Pepperpot, clinging on for dear life. BANG! Up into the cold night sky shot the rocket, the pole, the pipe *and* Mrs Pepperpot!

Round the bonfire everyone suddenly stopped shouting. A thin woman in a shawl whispered to her neighbour:

'I thought I saw someone sitting on that stick!'

Her neighbour, who was even thinner and wore two shawls, whispered back, 'It could have been a witch!' and they both shuddered. But from behind them came a man's voice:

'Oh, it couldn't be her, could it?' It was Mr Pepperpot who had just left off working and had taken a ride up to the mountain to have a look at the bonfire. Now he swung himself on his bicycle again and raced home as fast as he could go,

muttering all the way, 'Let her be at home; oh, please let her be at home!' When he reached the house and opened the door his hand was shaking.

There stood Mrs Pepperpot, quite her normal size and with no sign of a broomstick. She was decorating his birthday cake and on the table, neatly laid on a little cloth, was the precious pipe with its silver band.

'Many Happy Returns of the Day!' said Mrs Pepperpot. 'Come and have your meal now. Then you can put on a clean shirt and take your wife to dance all night at the bonfire party!'

'Anything you say!' said Mr Pepperpot; he was so relieved she hadn't gone off with the witches of Midsummer's Eve.

The Little Mouse
who was Very Clever

THERE was once a little mouse called Squeak, who sat behind the door in his mousehole, waiting for his mother to come home from the larder with some food.

Suddenly there was a knock at the door.

'Who is that?' asked little Squeak.

'Peep, peep, let me in, it's your mother,' said a voice outside, but it didn't sound a mousy sort of voice.

'Why are you knocking at our door?'

'I forgot to take the key,' said the voice.

'We don't use a key for this door,' said the little

mouse. 'It's bolted on the inside and I'm not opening it for *you*!'

Whoever it was went away and Squeak waited for some time before there came another knock.

'Who is that?' asked Squeak.

'It's Peter,' said a voice, but it didn't sound like Peter, the little boy who lived in the house.

'Why are you knocking at our door?'

'Because you've been using my shawl for your bed,' said the voice.

'If you're a little boy, you won't want a shawl,' said Squeak. 'I'm not opening the door for you!'

After he had waited some time there was another knock.

'Who is that?' he asked.

'Peter's mother,' came the reply; 'let me in.'

'Why are you knocking at our door?'

'Because I think you must have hidden my braces down your hole,' said the voice, which sounded rather purry for a lady.

'If you're Peter's mother,' said little Squeak, 'I'm sure you don't need braces. I'm not opening the door for *you*!'

Again he had to wait a long time before the next knock.

'Who is that?' said Squeak.

'This is Peter's father,' said a voice that was very croaky. 'Let me in at once!'

'Why are you knocking at our door?' asked the little mouse.

'My tail went in the honey-pot and I want you to clean it.'

'If you are Peter's father,' said Squeak, 'why have you got a tail? I'm not opening the door for *you!*'

After that there was a long, long silence, and then at last there was a tiny little knock.

'Who is that?' asked Squeak.

'It's your mother, darling.'

But the little mouse wanted to make quite sure:

'Why are you knocking at our door?'

'Because I want my clever Squeak to unbolt it as he always does,' said the voice. Then he knew it was his mother, and the little mouse, who was too clever to be tricked by a cat with many voices, unbolted the door and let his mother in.

And because he'd been so clever his mother gave him an extra large lump of cheese for his supper.

Mrs Pepperpot's Birthday

IT was Mrs Pepperpot's birthday, so she had asked her neighbours in to coffee at three o'clock. All day she had been scrubbing and polishing, and now it was ten minutes to three and she was putting the final touches to the strawberry layer cake on the kitchen table. As she stood balancing the last strawberry on a spoon, she suddenly felt herself shrinking, not slowly as she sometimes did, but so fast that she didn't even have time to put the strawberry on a plate. It rolled on to the floor and Mrs Pepperpot tumbled after it. But she quickly picked herself up and jumped into the cat's basket. Puss was a bit surprised, but allowed her to snuggle down with the kittens. In her black-and-white-striped skirt and white blouse, she hoped the guests would take her for one of the cat-family, until the magic wore off and she could be her real size again. For you may remember that Mrs Pepperpot never liked anyone to see her when she was tiny.

There was a knock at the door, and, when it wasn't answered, Sarah from South Farm walked into the little front hall, carrying a huge bunch of lilac.

'Many Happy Returns of the Day!' said Sarah. There was no reply, so she peered into the kitchen, thinking Mrs Pepperpot might be in there, though, naturally, she didn't look in the cat-basket. Somehow she managed to knock over the flower-vase on the hall table, and the water spilled on the tablecloth and on to the floor.

'Oh dear, oh dear!' thought Sarah. 'I shall have to mop up that before anybody notices.'

But at that moment there was another knock at

the door. So Sarah ran into the kitchen and hid in a cupboard.

In came Norah from North Farm, and she was carrying a very nice tablecloth.

'Many Happy Returns!' she said, but as she got no answer, she looked round for Mrs Pepperpot, and her parcel swept the vase off the table on to the floor.

'That's bad!' thought Norah. 'I must put it back before anybody comes.'

But before she could do it there was another knock on the door and Norah hurried into the bedroom and crept under the bed.

Esther from East Farm came in, carrying a handsome glass bowl for Mrs Pepperpot. When she had said 'Many Happy Returns!' and no one

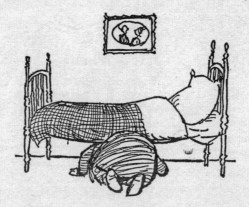

answered, she walked straight into the living-room. Carrying the bowl in front of her, she didn't notice the vase on the floor and put her foot straight on it. There was a nasty crunch and there it lay, in smithereens!

'Goodness gracious, what have I done?' thought Esther. 'Perhaps if I hide behind this curtain no one will know who did it!' So she quickly wrapped herself in one of the curtains.

At that moment the clock struck three, and the magic wore off; there was Mrs Pepperpot as large as life, walking through the kitchen. 'Coo-ee!' she called. 'You can all come out now!'

So Sarah stepped out of the cupboard, Norah crawled from under the bed, while Esther un-wrapped herself from the curtain in the living-room.

At first they looked a bit sheepish, but then they said 'Many Happy Returns!' all over again and they had a good laugh, while Mrs Pepperpot swept up the broken vase, threw away the dead flowers and put the wet tablecloth in the wash-tub.

Then she thanked them for their fine presents; the table was spread with Norah's tablecloth, Esther's glass bowl was filled with fresh water, and

the huge bunch of lilac that Sarah had brought was put into it.

After that Mrs Pepperpot brought in the coffee and cakes and they all sat down to enjoy themselves. But on the strawberry layer cake there was one strawberry missing.

'You see,' said Mrs Pepperpot, when they asked her what had happened to it, 'my *first* visitor this afternoon was the little old woman who shrinks and she was so tiny today that one strawberry was all she could manage to eat. So I gave her that and a thimble of milk to wash it down.'

'Didn't you ask her to stay, so that we could see her?' asked Sarah, for they were all very curious about the little old woman who shrank, and nobody thereabouts had ever seen her.

'She was sorry, she said, but she was in a tearing hurry; she had some business with a mouse, her night watchman or something. But she told me to tell you she did enjoy our little game of hide-and-seek!'

How the King Learned to Eat Porridge

THERE was once a king who was wise and good and mighty and rich, but he had one fault. Not a very big fault, mind you, but annoying enough. And do you know what it was?

He would not eat porridge.

Now this wouldn't have mattered so much if he had kept it to himself. After all, a king has so many other things to eat. But he was an honest king, so he could not lie, and he told both the government and the people that he did not like porridge.

'I detest porridge!' he declared. 'It tastes of glue and tufts of wool. Ugh!'

And when the people of his realm heard that they wouldn't eat porridge either. They wanted to be like the king – especially the children, who thought it was wonderful not to eat porridge, and whooped with delight. On the national flag-day they walked in the procession carrying big banners saying 'Long Live the King! Down with Porridge!'

But far up in the mountains there lived a

peasant with his daughter, and they had only one tiny field of their own. On this field they grew oats, and their whole livelihood depended on it. So when everyone stopped buying oats they made less and less money.

'This can't go on!' said the peasant's daughter one day. 'People not eating porridge like this. I shall have to go to the palace and give that stupid king a piece of my mind!'

'Take care, my child, you might make the king angry,' said her father.

'He'd better take care himself,' she answered, 'or *I* might get angry.' And she slung a bag of oatmeal over her shoulder and set off for the palace.

In the palace garden she met a man, but the country girl did not know he was really the king.

'Where are you off to?' asked the man.

'I'm going to the palace to teach the king to eat porridge,' she answered.

This made the man laugh. 'If you can do that,' he said, 'you're a very clever girl!' Then he went into the royal kitchen and told the royal cook that he could take the day off, as a country girl had come to town to teach him, the king, to eat porridge.

Next day, when the king was at breakfast, the peasant's daughter brought in a big steaming bowl of porridge. She was a little taken aback when she saw who the man was she had spoken to in the garden. But the king smiled at her and said:

'Come along now, you must teach me to eat this porridge of yours.'

'Oh no,' she said, 'not after making such a fool of myself, I couldn't. Anyway, I don't suppose you even know which hand to hold the spoon in?'

'I think I do,' said the king, and picked up the spoon in his right hand.

'Just as I thought!' said the girl. 'Never in all my life have I seen anyone eat porridge with the right hand!'

'All right,' said the king, 'I'll try with my left hand.'

'That's better,' said the girl, 'but I've never seen anyone with a bowl of porridge on the table while they sat on a chair to eat it. Get up on the table and put the bowl on the chair in the proper manner!'

The king was beginning to enjoy himself. First he got up on the table and then he tried to set the bowl on the chair. But this was not so easy; he nearly lost his balance several times before he managed it.

'There, now you can start eating,' said the girl.

The king held the spoon in his left hand and bent down to the bowl. It was awkward, but he succeeded at last in getting a spoonful up to his mouth and swallowing it.

'Just a minute,' said the girl, 'you have to hold your left ear with your right hand while you're eating.'

'I expect I can manage that too,' said the king, and balanced another spoonful up to his mouth.

'That's only two spoonfuls,' she said. 'Wait till you get to the bottom of the bowl; that's when it gets really difficult.'

'Don't worry, I'll do it!' said the king, and, do you know, he didn't give in till he had scraped the bowl clean!

'There you are!' he shouted proudly.

'There you are yourself!' said the girl. 'Now I have taught the king to eat porridge!'

At first the king was a little put out that she had tricked him in this way. But then he had to laugh.

'You're a very cunning little girl,' he said. 'I almost think I'll marry you – that is, if you're willing?'

'I might as well,' said the girl.

*

So they were married, and at the wedding a huge pot of hot, steaming porridge was set up in the middle of the market place, and the king commanded his people, including the whole court and all his ministers, to come and learn how to eat porridge.

The queen stood on a high tribune to teach them, and they all laughed and enjoyed themselves like anything. But when they had had their lesson the queen said:

'Now I know you can all eat porridge; so from this day on you may sit on your chairs and put your porridge bowls on the table and eat it the way you do with any other food.'

But many people, especially the children, preferred the way the queen had taught them and went on doing it – secretly.

Mrs Pepperpot Turns Fortune-Teller

EVERY morning when Mr Pepperpot goes off to work Mrs Pepperpot stands at the window and watches him till he disappears round the bend to the main road. Then she settles in the chair by the

kitchen table, picks up her empty coffee cup and starts reading her fortune in it.

Now you probably didn't know that Mrs Pepperpot could read fortunes in a cup. Well, she can; she can tell from the way the coffee grounds lie what road she will take that day and whether she will meet joy or sorrow before nightfall. Sometimes she sees the shape of a heart in the cup and that means she will have a new sweetheart. But that makes Mrs Pepperpot laugh, for to her it means she will probably get a new pet to look after – perhaps a poor little bird with a broken wing or a stray kitten on her doorstep, getting tamer and tamer as it laps up the food and milk she gives it.

But if the grounds form a cross she knows she must watch her step, for that means she will break something; it could be when she is washing up or when she is scrubbing the floor. If she sees a clear drop of coffee running down the side of the cup that means she will hurt herself in some way and will need not only a bandage but maybe a doctor as well. And so it goes on; there are many more signs that she can read, but she only does it for herself, never for other people, even if they ask her. It's just an amusement, she says, something to while away the time when she is at home alone all day.

Well, this day – it was a Friday too – Mrs Pepperpot had planned to give the house a good clean out and then she was going to bake a cake for Mr Pepperpot. Apart from that she was just going to take it easy for a change. So, when she had watched her husband turn the corner, she picked up their two coffee cups and was just about to put them in the sink. But she stopped herself.

'There, what am I doing? I nearly forgot to have a look at my fortune for today!' So she took one of the cups back to the table and sat down. 'Let's see, now,' she said and turned the cup round and round in her hand. 'Oh dear, oh dear!' she exclaimed, 'what's this I see? A big cross? I shall have to mind how I go today and no mistake!'

At that very moment she shrank, and in no time at all she was no bigger than the coffee cup and both she and the cup fell off the chair on to the floor.

'That was a bit of a come-down!' she said, and felt both her arms and her legs to see if there were any bones broken. But when she found she was still all in one piece she lay still for a moment, not daring to look at the cup. For it was one of her best ones, and she was sure it must have been broken by the fall.

At last she said to herself, 'I suppose I shall have to take a look.' And when she did she found to her great surprise that the cup was not even cracked or chipped.

But she was still worried. 'If that isn't it there'll be something else for me to break today,' she said miserably as she squatted down to look into the cup, for it was lying on its side.

'Oh me, oh my!' she cried. 'If this isn't my unlucky day!' She had caught sight of a large clear drop on the side of the cup. 'This means tears, but I wonder what will make me cry?'

Suddenly there was a loud BANG! inside the kitchen cupboard. Mrs Pepperpot nearly jumped out of her skin with fright.

'There! Now isn't that just like Mr P., setting a mousetrap in the cupboard, although he knows it's not necessary now that I have a mouse for a night watchman. It's only now and again that a baby mouse gets into the cupboard by mistake – before he's learned the mouse rules. It's not as if they *mean* to do any damage, so it's silly to take any notice. I wonder if I dare open the door a little to see what's happened? I suppose I'd better; the little thing might just have caught its tail and I could free it. But, of course, it might be worse than that; the cup said tears, and tears it will be, no doubt!'

So Mrs Pepperpot went over to the cupboard and pulled gently at the door. But she closed her eyes to keep back the tears which were ready to come at any moment. When she had the door opened enough to look in she opened first one eye, then the other, and then she flopped down on the floor, clapping her hands on her knees, and burst out laughing.

Right enough, the trap had snapped, but there was nothing in it. Instead two baby mice were happily playing just beside it with two empty cotton-reels. Mrs Pepperpot thought it was the funniest sight she'd ever seen.

'Hullo, Mrs Pepperpot!' squealed one of the baby mice. 'Have you shrunk again?'

'We hoped you would!' said the other one,
''cos my brother and I had never seen you small
before, and Granny said we could come in here
and have a peep – just in case you shrunk. We
weren't being naughty – just playing cars – and
then we bumped into that nasty thing which went
snap over there.'

'Will you play with us?' asked the first little
mouse. 'You sit in the car and we'll pull you
along.'

And when Mrs Pepperpot looked closer she
saw that the baby mice had fixed a matchbox over
the cotton-reels and the whole contraption really
moved.

'Let's go!' shouted Mrs Pepperpot, and jumped
into the box.

So they played at cars, taking turns to sit in the

matchbox, and Mrs Pepperpot laughed while the
baby mice squealed with delight, till, all of a
sudden, they heard a scratching sound above
them.

'That's enough, children!' called granny
mouse, whose head had appeared in a hole in the
back wall. 'The cat's on top of the cupboard and
the door is open!'

Before you could say 'knife' the two baby mice
had disappeared through the hole, squeaking
'Thanks for the game!' as they went.

'Thank you!' said Mrs Pepperpot, and stepped
out of the cupboard to see what that cat was up to.

There she was, standing on top of the cupboard
waving her tail expectantly when Mrs Pepperpot
came out. But Mrs Pepperpot was not standing
any nonsense; she shouted at the cat: 'What are
you doing up there? You get down at once or I'll
teach you a lesson as soon as I grow again!
Maybe it's you who are going to break something
for me today? Yes, I can feel it in my bones. I
know if I have another look in that cup there'll be
more calamity there for me.'

By now she was just as worked up as she had
been before her little game with the mice. But she
couldn't resist having another look in the cup.

'Goodness gracious!' she cried. 'It's just as I thought, doctor and bandages, ambulances and everything! As if I hadn't trouble enough already! Down you get, cat, and make it quick!'

'All right! Keep your hair on,' said the cat. 'I was only doing my duty when I heard a suspicious noise in the cupboard. I'm coming down now.'

'Mind how you go! Be careful! I don't want anything broken. I'll stand here below and direct you,' said Mrs Pepperpot.

'Anybody would think I'd never jumped off a cupboard before, and I'm not in the habit of breaking things,' answered the cat, as he made his way gingerly past a big china bowl. But just on the edge of the cupboard lay a large pair of scissors, and neither the cat nor Mrs Pepperpot had seen them.

Mrs Pepperpot was busy with her warnings: 'Mind that bowl!' she shouted, standing right beneath those scissors.

The cat was being as careful as she could, but her tail brushed against the scissors, sending them flying, point downwards, to the floor. There they stood quivering!

Mrs Pepperpot had just managed to jump out of the way, but now she was too frightened to move. 'So that was it!' she stammered at last.

She felt herself all over again, for this time she was *sure* she must be hurt. But she couldn't find as much as a scratch!

A moment later she was her normal size. So she pulled the scissors out of the floor and lifted the cat down out of harm's way. Then she set to work cleaning the house and just had time to bake her cake before she heard her husband at the door.

But what a state he was in! The tears were pouring out of his eyes because of the bitter wind outside, and anyway he had a bad cold. One hand he was holding behind his back: he had fallen off his bicycle, had broken his cycle lamp and cut his hand on the glass!

As she hurriedly searched for something to tie round his hand, Mrs Pepperpot thought how odd it was that it was Mr Pepperpot who had tears in his eyes; it was Mr Pepperpot that had broken something, and had hurt himself so that he had to have a bandage on. Very odd indeed!

But if you think this cured Mrs Pepperpot of reading her fortune in a coffee cup you are very much mistaken. The only thing is, she *does* take care not to pick up the wrong cup and read her husband's fortune instead of her own.

The Fairy-Tale Boy

ONCE upon a time there was a little boy who said to his mother, 'I want to go out into the world and kill a dragon, and then I'll bring you back all the gold.'

His mother answered: 'But what about the princess? Won't you set her free as well, pet?'

'I suppose so,' said George, for that was his name, 'as long as I don't have to marry her; 'cos you know I don't like girls.'

'Very well, dear; good luck!' said his mother.

'Oh, but you mustn't just say "good luck!" You have to give me food and drink for the journey. I'm going to sit down by the side of the road and start eating, and then an old woman will come or a dwarf, or something like that, and they'll be hungry, and I'll give them all my food, 'cos then they'll help me, you know, to find the way to the dragon and all that.'

'All right, pet, you shall have some food for the journey,' said his mother, and she put three sandwiches in a tin and put them in a little knapsack with a bottle of milk.

So George went out into the world to kill the dragon. And when he had walked a little he came to a road crossing and there he sat down and opened his knapsack and took out a sandwich.

'I 'spect an old woman will come along in a minute, and she'll ask me for food. Then afterwards she's sure to show me the way to the dragon,' he said to himself.

No sooner had he thought of this than an old woman *did* come round the corner, walking slowly

towards him. When she reached the place where he was sitting she stopped and fixed her eyes on George's sandwich.

'Good afternoon,' said George, and held out his hand with the sandwich in it.

'Good afternoon, my boy,' said the woman; 'you shouldn't play with your food like that.'

'I'm *not* playing with my food,' said George indignantly. 'I'm giving it to you. Aren't you hungry?'

'Of course not,' said the woman. 'I have my lunch before I go out, and so should you, young fellow, and not drag it about with you, leaving dirty bits of paper behind and egg-shells and I don't know what. Ugh!' And with that she walked off and left George holding his sandwich.

George sat staring after her for a bit.

'Oh well,' he said, 'I suppose there'll be others coming along. She wasn't the right kind of fairy-tale woman, anyway. I'd better eat this sandwich myself while I'm waiting.'

While he was munching the bread he heard a scuffling noise behind the hedge. It was the squirrel.

'Hullo, squirrel! Would you like something to eat?' said George, and threw the second sandwich

into the hedge. But the squirrel took fright and bounded away towards a wood.

'Perhaps it wants me to follow it,' thought George. So he picked up his knapsack and walked after the squirrel to the wood. The squirrel, meanwhile, stayed quite still, as if it were really waiting for him, and George was now quite certain that it was going to show him the way to the dragon. When he got quite close the squirrel started leaping from branch to branch and George began to run, stumbling over sticks and stumps, further and further into the wood, until at last they came to a little stream. Here the squirrel jumped lightly from a tree on one side of the stream to another tree on the other side. But George stopped; the stream was too deep for him to wade across, and he was afraid he might drown. So he very sensibly stayed where he was.

Instead he sat down by the edge of the stream and took out his last sandwich. Just then he saw a fish swimming by.

'P'raps you're the one who is going to help me,' he said, and threw the last sandwich into the water. But the fish dodged under a stone and the sandwich floated away down the stream.

George jumped up and followed the bobbing

sandwich to see where it would go. Soon the stream widened and ran into a pool, and there on the bank stood a big boy watching a fishing-line.

'Don't make so much noise!' said the big boy. 'You'll frighten the fish away!'

'Sorry!' said George. 'Would you like some milk?' he asked.

'Milk? Are you off your head? How d'you expect me to drink milk while I'm fishing? You scram out of here and be quick about it!'

Well, there was nothing for it; George had to make himself scarce, but he was beginning to feel a little sad. His adventure wasn't turning out quite as he had planned. He sat down in a patch of bilberries and drank up his bottle of milk himself. Then he lay down and took a little nap.

When he woke up there was a little girl standing there, watching him.

'Hullo!' said George.

'Hullo!' said the little girl. 'You looked so nice, lying there asleep; just like my cousin! What a smart sandwich tin you've got; I haven't got one like that with Donald Duck on it.'

'Got it for my birthday,' said George. He was suddenly feeling very hungry, but there was nothing left to eat.

'Are you very hungry?' asked the little girl. 'I can give you some food, if you like. I'm bilberrying, you see, so I've brought a picnic lunch – look! Sausages and strawberry jelly; it's jolly good!'

'Thank you very much,' said George, and he ate up two sausages and all the jelly that was left.

The little girl stood watching him, and when he had finished she said, 'Now you will have to save me from the dragon.'

'Dragon?' George gulped and the last bit of jelly went down the wrong way.

'Of course,' she said. 'When you've eaten the princess's food you must kill the dragon. It is lying just down there in the bushes.'

'All right, I'm ready!' said George in his most manly voice. He was a *little* afraid when he started walking over to the bushes. But he picked up a good stout stick – sorry, I mean sword – and

smacked the dragon right on the nose. Wham! Afterwards he hacked it into several pieces and then he jumped on them to make quite sure it was dead.

'It's quite safe now, Princess!' he said to the little girl. 'You can come out now!'

'Oh, thank you, St George!' she said. 'Now you can marry me if you like – unless I marry my cousin, of course.'

'You marry your cousin,' said George. 'I don't mind.'

'All right. But you can come home with me if you like, and have some more jelly.'

'No thanks, Princess,' said George. 'You see, I have to look for the gold now that I've killed the dragon.'

And do you know? Under the tree-stump – sorry, I mean the dragon – George found a heap of beautiful pebbles that shone in the sun like silver when he ran them through his hands. George put them all in his knapsack and was very pleased with his treasure even though it wasn't gold.

After all, you can't expect to find gold under the first dragon you kill.

The Ski-Race

MRS PEPPERPOT has done a lot of things in her life, and most of them I've told you about already. But now I must tell you how she went ski-racing one day last winter.

*

Mr Pepperpot had decided to go in for the annual local ski-race. He had been a pretty good skier when he was young, so he said to Mrs Pepperpot:

'I don't see why I shouldn't have a go this year; I feel more fit than I have for many years.'

'That's right, husband, you do that,' said Mrs Pepperpot, 'and if you win the cup you'll get your favourite ginger cake when you come home.'

So Mr Pepperpot put his name down, and when the day came he put on his white anorak and blue cap with a bobble on the top and strings under his chin. He slung his skis over his shoulders and said he would wax them when he got to the starting point.

'Righto! Best of luck!' said Mrs Pepperpot. She

was already greasing the cake-tin and stoking the stove for her baking.

'Thanks, wife,' said Mr Pepperpot and went off. It was not before he had turned by the main road that Mrs Pepperpot caught sight of his tin of wax which he had left on the sideboard.

'What a dunderhead that man is!' exclaimed Mrs Pepperpot. 'Now I shall have to go after him, I suppose; otherwise his precious skis are more likely to go backwards than forwards and there'll be no cup in this house today.'

So Mrs Pepperpot flung her shawl round her shoulders and trotted up the road as fast as she could with the tin of wax. When she got near the starting point there was a great crowd gathered. She dodged in and out to try and find her husband, but everyone seemed to be wearing white anoraks and blue caps. At last she saw a pair of sticks stuck in the snow with a blue cap hanging from the top. She could see the initials P.P. sewn in red thread inside.

'That must be his cap,' thought Mrs Pepperpot. 'Those are his initials, Peter Pepperpot. I sewed them on myself in red thread like that. I'll just drop the wax in the cap; then he'll find it when he comes to pick up his sticks.'

As she bent forward to put the wax in the cap she accidentally knocked it off the stick and at that moment she shrank so quickly that it was she who fell into the cap, while the tin of wax rolled out into the snow!

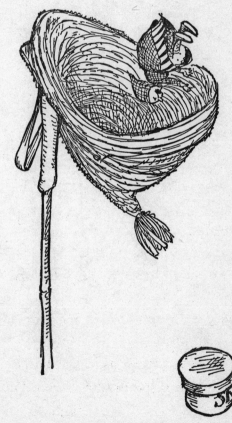

'No harm done,' thought Mrs Pepperpot; 'when he comes along he'll see me in his cap. Then he can put me down somewhere out of the way of the race. And as soon as I grow large again I can go home.'

But a moment later a big hand reached down, snatched up the cap and crammed it over a mop of thick hair. The strings were firmly tied and Mrs Pepperpot was trapped!

'Oh well!' she thought. 'I'd better not say anything before the race starts.' For she knew Mr Pepperpot hated to think anybody might get to know about her shrinking.

'Number 46!' she heard the starter shout, 'on your mark, get set, go!' And Number 46, with Mrs Pepperpot in his cap, glided off to a smooth start.

'Somebody must have lent him some wax,' she thought; 'there's nothing wrong with his skis, anyway.' Then from under the cap she shouted, 'Don't overdo it, now, or you'll have no breath left for the spurt at the end!'

She could feel the skier slow up a little. 'I suppose you know who's under your cap?' she added. 'You had forgotten the wax, so I brought it along. Only I fell into your cap instead of the wax.'

Mrs Pepperpot now felt the skier's head turn round to see if anyone was talking to him from behind.

'It's me, you fool!' said Mrs Pepperpot. 'I've shrunk again. You'll have to put me off by the lane to our house – you pass right by, remember?'

But the skier had stopped completely now.

'Come on, man, get a move on!' shouted Mrs Pepperpot. 'They'll all be passing you!'

'Is it . . . is it true that you're the little old woman who shrinks to the size of a pepperpot?'

'Of course – you know that!' laughed Mrs Pepperpot.

'Am *I* married to *you*? Is it *my* wife who shrinks?'

'Yes, yes, but hurry now!'

'No,' said the skier, 'if that's how it is I'm not going on with the race at all.'

'Rubbish!' shouted Mrs Pepperpot. 'You *must* go on! I put a cake in the oven before I went out and if it's scorched it'll be all your fault!'

But the skier didn't budge.

'Maybe you'd like me to pop out of your cap and show myself to everybody? Any minute now I might go back to my full size and then the cap will burst and the whole crowd will see who is married to the shrinking woman. Come on, now!

With any luck you may just do it, but there's no time to lose; HURRY!'

This worked; the skier shot off at full speed, helping himself to huge strides with his sticks. 'Fore!' he shouted as he sped past the other skiers. But when they came to the refreshment stall Mrs Pepperpot could smell the lovely hot soup, and she thought her husband deserved a break. 'We're well up now,' she called. 'You could take a rest.'

The skier slowed down to a stop and Mrs Pepperpot could hear there were many people standing round him. 'Well done!' they said. 'You're very well placed. But what are you looking so worried about? Surely you're not frightened of the last lap, are you?'

'No, no, nothing like that!' said the skier. 'It's this cap of mine – I'm dead scared of my cap!'

But the people patted him on the back and told him not to worry, he had a good chance of winning.

Under the cap Mrs Pepperpot was getting restless again. 'That's enough of that!' she called. 'We'll have to get on now!'

The people who stood nearest heard the voice and wondered who spoke. The woman who ladled out the soup said, 'Probably some loud-speaker.'

And Mrs Pepperpot couldn't help laughing. 'Nearer the truth than you think!' she thought. Then she called out again, 'Come on, husband, put that spurt on, and let's see if we can make it!'

And the skis shot away again, leaping many yards each time the sticks struck into the snow. Very soon Mrs Pepperpot could hear the sound of clapping and cheering.

'What do we do now?' whispered the skier in a miserable voice. 'Can you last another minute? Then I can throw the cap off under the fir trees just before we reach the finishing line.'

'Yes, that will be all right,' said Mrs Pepperpot. And, as the skis sped down the last slope, the strings were untied and the cap flew through the air, landing safely under the fir trees.

When Mrs Pepperpot had rolled over and over many times she found herself growing big once more. So she got up, shook the snow off her skirt and walked quietly home to her house. From the cheering in the distance she was sure her husband had won the cup.

The cake was only a little bit burnt on the top when she took it out of the oven, so she cut off the black part and gave it to the cat. Then she whipped some cream to put on top and made a steaming pot of coffee to have ready for her champion husband.

Sure enough, Mr Pepperpot soon came home – *without* the cup. 'I forgot to take the wax,' he said, 'so I didn't think it was worth going in for the race. But I watched it, and you should have seen Paul Petersen today; I've never seen him run like that in all my born days. All the same, he looked very queer, as if he'd seen a ghost or something. When it was over he kept talking about his wife and his cap, and he wasn't satisfied till he'd telephoned his house and made sure his wife had been there all the time, watching the race on television.'

Then Mrs Pepperpot began to laugh. And ever since, when she's feeling sad or things are not going just right, all she has to do is to remember the day she went ski-racing in the wrong cap, and then she laughs and laughs and laughs.

Mrs Pepperpot and the Moose

IT was winter-time, and Mrs Pepperpot was having trouble getting water. The tap in her kitchen ran slower and slower, until one day it just dripped and then stopped altogether. The well was empty.

'Ah well,' thought Mrs Pepperpot, 'it won't be the first time I've had this kind of trouble, and it won't be the last. But with two strong arms and a good sound bucket, not to mention the lucky chance that there's another well down by the forest fence, we'll soon fix that.'

So she put on her husband's old winter coat and a pair of thick gloves and fetched a pick-axe from the wood-shed. Then she trudged through the snow down the hill, to where there was a dip by the forest fence. She swept the snow away and started breaking a hole in the ice with the pick-axe. Chips of ice flew everywhere as Mrs Pepperpot hacked away, not looking to left or right. She made such a noise that she never heard the sound of breaking twigs, nor the snorting that was coming from the other side of the fence.

But there he was; a huge moose with great big

antlers, not moving at all, but staring angrily at Mrs Pepperpot. Suddenly he gave a very loud snort and leaped over the fence, butting Mrs Pepperpot from behind, so that she went head-first into a pile of snow!

'What the dickens!' cried Mrs Pepperpot as she scrambled to her feet. But by that time the moose was back on the other side of the fence. When she saw what it was that had pushed her over, Mrs

Pepperpot lost no time in scrambling up the hill and into her house, locking the door behind her. Then she peeped out of the kitchen window to see if the moose was still there. He was.

'You wait, you great big brute!' said Mrs Pepperpot. 'I'll give you a fright you won't forget!'

She put on a black rain-cape and a battered old hat, and in her hand she carried a big stick. Then she crept out of the door and hid round the corner of the house.

The moose was quietly nibbling the bark off the trees and seemed to be taking no notice of her.

Suddenly she stormed down the hill, shouting, 'Woollah, Woollah, Woollah!' like a Red Indian, the black rain-cape flapping round her and the stick waving in the air. The moose *should* have been frightened, but he just took one look at the whirling thing coming towards him, leaped the fence and headed straight for it!

Poor Mrs Pepperpot! All she could do was to rush back indoors again as fast as she knew how.

'Now what shall I do?' she wondered. 'I must have water to cook my potatoes and do my washing-up, and a little cup of coffee wouldn't come amiss after all this excitement. Perhaps if I were to put on my old man's trousers and take his gun out . . . I could pretend to aim it; that might scare him off.'

So she put on the trousers and took out the gun; but this was the silliest idea she had had yet, because, before she was half-way down the hill, that moose came pounding towards her on his great long legs. She never had time to point the gun. Worse still, she dropped it in her efforts to keep the trousers up and run back to the house at the same time. When the moose saw her disappear indoors, he turned and stalked down the hill again, but this time he didn't jump back over the fence, but stayed by the well, as if he were guarding it.

'Ah well,' said Mrs Pepperpot, 'I suppose I shall have to fill the bucket with snow and melt it to get the water I need. That moose is clearly not afraid of anything.'

So she took her bucket and went outside. But just as she was bending down to scoop up the snow, she turned small! But this time the magic worked quicker than usual, and somehow she managed to tumble into the bucket which was lying on its side. The bucket started to roll down the hill; faster and faster it went, and poor Mrs Pepperpot was seeing stars as she bumped round and round inside.

Just above the dip near the well a little mound
jutted out, and here the bucket made a leap into
space. 'This is the end of me!' thought Mrs
Pepperpot. She waited for the bump, but it didn't
come! Instead the bucket seemed to be floating
through the air, over the fence and right into the
forest. If she had had time to think, Mrs Pepperpot
would have known that the moose had somehow
caught the bucket on one of his antlers, but it is
not so easy to think when you're swinging between
heaven and earth.

At last the bucket got stuck on a branch and the moose thundered on through the undergrowth. Mrs Pepperpot lay there panting, trying to get her breath back. She had no idea where she was. But then she heard: 'Chuck, chuck! Chuck, chuck!' – the chattering of a squirrel as he ran down the tree-trunk over her head.

'Hullo!' said the squirrel, 'if it isn't Mrs Pepperpot! Out for a walk, or something?'

'Not exactly a *walk*,' said Mrs Pepperpot, 'but I've had a free ride, though I don't know who gave it to me.'

'That was the King of the Moose,' said the squirrel. 'I saw him gallop past with a wild look in his eyes. It's the first time I have ever seen him afraid, I can tell you that. He is so stupid and so stuck-up you wouldn't believe it. All he thinks of is fighting; he goes for anything and anybody – the bigger the better. But you seem to have given him the fright of his life.'

'I'm glad I managed it in the end,' said Mrs Pepperpot, 'and now I'd be gladder still if I knew how to get myself home.'

But she needn't have worried, because at that moment she felt herself grow large again, and the next thing she knew she had broken the branch and was lying on the ground. She picked herself and her bucket up and started walking home. But when she got to the fence she took a turn down to the well to fill the bucket.

When she stood up she looked back towards the forest, and there, sure enough, stood the moose, blinking at her. But Mrs Pepperpot was no longer afraid of him. All she had to do was to rattle that bucket a little, and the big creature shook his head and disappeared silently into the forest.

From that day on Mrs Pepperpot had no trouble fetching water from the well by the forest fence.

Some other Young Puffins

LUCKY DIP *Ruth Ainsworth*

Stories from the BBC's *Listen With Mother*. Seven of the ever-popular *Charles* stories are included. (Also available in Initial Teaching Alphabet edition.)

THE TEN TALES OF SHELLOVER *Ruth Ainsworth*

The Black Hens, the Dog and the Cat didn't like Shellover the tortoise at first, until they discovered what wonderful stories he told.

LITTLE PETE STORIES *Leila Berg*

More favourites from *Listen With Mother*, about a small boy who plays mostly by himself. Illustrated by Peggy Fortnum.

PADDINGTON AT LARGE *Michael Bond*

PADDINGTON ABROAD

PADDINGTON MARCHES ON

PADDINGTON AT WORK

Named after the railway station on which he was found, Paddington is an intelligent, well-meaning, likeable bear who somehow always manages to get into trouble. Illustrated by Peggy Fortnum.

THE CASTLE OF YEW *Lucy M. Boston*

Joseph visits the magic garden where the yew trees are shaped like castles – and finds himself shrunk small enough to crawl inside one.

THE HAPPY ORPHELINE *Natalie Savage Carlson*

The twenty little orphaned girls who live with Madame Flattot are terrified of being adopted because they are so happy.

FIVE DOLLS IN A HOUSE *Helen Clare*

A little girl called Elizabeth finds a way of making herself small and visits her dolls in their own house.

TELL ME A STORY *Eileen Colwell*
TELL ME ANOTHER STORY
TIME FOR A STORY
Stories, verses, and finger plays for children of 3 to 6, collected by the greatest living expert on the art of children's story-telling.

MY NAUGHTY LITTLE SISTER *Dorothy Edwards*
MY NAUGHTY LITTLE SISTER'S FRIENDS
These now famous stories were originally told by a mother to her own children. Ideal for reading aloud. For ages 4 to 8.

MISS HAPPINESS AND MISS FLOWER *Rumer Godden*
Nona was lonely far away from her home in India, and the two dainty Japanese dolls, Miss Happiness and Miss Flower, were lonely too. But once Nona started building them a proper Japanese house they all felt happier. Illustrated by Jean Primrose.

THE YOUNG PUFFIN BOOK OF VERSE *Barbara Ireson*
A deluge of poems about such fascinating subjects as birds and balloons, mice and moonshine, farmers and frogs, pigeons and pirates, especially chosen to please young people of four to eight. (*Original*)

THE STORY OF FERDINAND *Munro Leaf*
The endearing story of the adventures of the nicest bull there ever was – and it has a very happy ending.

MEET MARY KATE *Helen Morgan*
Charmingly told stories of a four-year-old's everyday life in the country. Illustrated by Shirley Hughes.

PUFFIN BOOK OF NURSERY RHYMES
Peter and Iona Opie
The first comprehensive collection of nursery rhymes to be produced as a paperback, prepared for Puffins by the leading authorities on children's lore. 220 pages, exquisitely illustrated on every page by Pauline Baynes. (*A Young Puffin Original.*)

LITTLE OLD MRS PEPPERPOT *Alf Prøysen*
MRS PEPPERPOT IN THE MAGIC WOOD
More gay little stories about the old woman who suddenly shrinks to the size of a pepperpot.

ROM-BOM-BOM AND OTHER STORIES *Antonia Ridge*
A collection of animal stories written by the distinguished children's author and broadcaster. For 4 to 8 year olds.

DEAR TEDDY ROBINSON *Joan G. Robinson*
MORE ABOUT TEDDY ROBINSON
Teddy Robinson was Deborah's teddy bear and such a very nice, friendly cuddly bear that he went everywhere with her and had even more adventures than she did.

THE ADVENTURES OF GALLDORA *Modwena Sedgwick*
NEW ADVENTURES OF GALLDORA
This lovable rag doll belonged to Marybell, who wasn't always very careful to look after her, so Galldora was always getting lost – in a field with a scarecrow, on top of a roof, and in all sorts of other strange places.

SOMETHING TO DO *Septima*
Suggestions for games to play and things to make and do each month, from January to December. It is designed to help mothers with young children at home. (*A Young Puffin Original.*)

SOMETHING TO MAKE *Felicia Law*
A varied and practical collection of things for children to make from odds and ends around the house with very little extra outlay, by an experienced teacher of art and handicrafts. For children of 6 up. (*Original*)

PONDER AND WILLIAM *Barbara Softly*
PONDER AND WILLIAM ON HOLIDAY
Ponder the panda looks after William's pyjamas and is a wonderful companion in these all-the-year-round adventures. Illustrated by Diana John. (*Young Puffin Originals.*)

CLEVER POLLY AND THE STUPID WOLF *Catherine Storr*
Clever Polly manages to think of lots of good ideas to stop the stupid wolf from eating her.

DANNY FOX *David Thompson*
Clever Danny Fox helps the Princess to marry the fisherman she loves, and comes safely home to his hungry family. (*A Young Puffin Original.*)

If you have enjoyed this book and would like to know about others which we publish, why not join the Puffin Club? You will be sent the Club magazine, *Puffin Post*, four times a year and a smart badge and membership book. You will also be able to enter all the competitions. Write for an application form to:

The Puffin Club Secretary
Penguin Books Ltd
Bath Road
Harmondsworth
Middlesex